CAKES

AND

MIRACLES

A PURIM TALE

For my son, Jeremy — B. D. G.

For my little boy, Fin — J. Z.

Marshall Cavendish Corporation, 99 White Plains Road, Tarrytown, NY 10591
www.marshallcavendish.us/kids

Library of Congress Cataloging-in-Publication Data

Goldin, Barbara Diamond.
 Cakes and miracles : a Purim tale / Barbara Diamond Goldin ; Jaime
Zollars. — 1st ed.
p. cm.
Summary: Young, blind Hershel finds that he has special gifts he can use
to help his mother during the Jewish holiday of Purim. Includes author's
notes about the holiday and its origins.
ISBN 978-0-7614-5701-5
[1. Purim—Fiction. 2. Blind—Fiction. 3. People with
disabilities—Fiction. 4. Judaism—Customs and practices—Fiction.]
I. Zollars, Jaime, ill. II. Title.   PZ7.G5674.Cak 2010   [E]—dc22
2009045205

Cakes and Miracles: A Purim Tale was published originally
by Viking Press in 1991. This new edition has a shortened
text and new illustrations.

The illustrations are rendered in collage and acrylic paint.
Book design by Becky Terhune
Editor: Margery Cuyler

Printed in China (E)
First edition
1 3 5 6 4 2

mc Marshall Cavendish
Children

CAKES AND MIRACLES

A PURIM TALE

by Barbara Diamond Goldin

illustrated by Jaime Zollars

MARSHALL CAVENDISH CHILDREN

Hershel was the only blind boy in his village. But his blindness did not keep him from going to school, or shaking pears from the neighbor's tree, or catching frogs in the river.

The river was Hershel's favorite place in the village. Besides frogs and water, there was mud to play in. He could make the mud do anything he wanted it to do. A poke here and he had a cave. A push there, he had a tunnel. He tried to wash the mud off his clothes before he went home, but he always missed a patch or two.

"You have to go to the river and get all muddy?" his mother, Basha, said when he came inside.

Hershel sighed. He did not mean to make extra work for his mother. Ever since his father died, she was busy enough trying to feed and clothe the two of them.

She sewed. She cleaned. She cooked. She baked. Especially in early spring, at Purim time, she baked. Then the three-cornered fat cakes called hamantashen sold well in the marketplace.

"This year, maybe I can sell enough hamantashen to buy two more chickens," Basha said hopefully.

"This year, maybe I can help you with the cakes," said Hershel.

"But you cannot see to make them," said Basha. "Do not worry, Hershel. You will help me in other ways, as you always do." And she patted his head lovingly.

That night, the night before Purim, Hershel climbed into his bed. After he said his bedtime prayer, he whispered, "If only I could see and help my mother more."

In the night, he had a dream. In his dream, Hershel saw the most beautiful winged angel descending a sparkling ladder. The angel bent down toward him.

"Make what you see," the angel said.

"But I haven't been able to see since I was sick," Hershel protested.

"You see when you close your eyes. You see in your dreams," the angel answered.

"It's true. I can see in my dreams," he whispered.

Hershel awoke and the angel was gone. But he remembered what the angel said.

Soon, he heard his mother stoking the stove. "Mother," he called out. "Good news! I can see. In my head. And I can help you with your cakes."

"Hershel, Hershel," said Basha, shaking her head sadly. "You wish you could see. I wish you could see. But how can a blind boy see? I can't let you play with the dough."

"I won't play, Mother. I'll make cakes. Or maybe something different. Cookies. Cookies in wonderful shapes."

"Shapes, too, Hershel! Such a good imagination my son has!"

After school, Hershel did his chores. He fetched. He carried. He cleaned pans, while his mother mixed and rolled, cut and baked.

At nightfall, Basha said, "I'll leave this batch of dough to roll and cut in the morning, Purim morning." And they went to synagogue to hear the chanting of the Megillah, the story of Queen Esther.

Hershel did not forget his noisemaker. Every child had one. And when the rabbi chanted the name of the villain, Haman, his voice was drowned by the shaking and rattling of the noisemakers. What fun Hershel had.

But that night, Hershel could not sleep. He went to the kitchen where his mother's hamantashen lay.

He felt for the bowl filled with dough and took a piece with his hands. The cool smoothness made him think of the mud by the river.

Hershel kneaded the dough. He formed a bird and a fish and a goblet. As he worked, he found it easier and easier to shape the cookies so they matched the images dancing in his head.

As the night turned to day, his mother awoke.

"What are you doing, Hershel?" she demanded. "I told you not to play with the dough."

Then she saw Hershel's cookies.

"But . . . but . . . they are beautiful, Hershel. How can a boy who cannot see . . ."

"But I can see," Hershel interrupted. "When I close my eyes, I see."

"Truly a miracle!" Basha said, and took Hershel's face tenderly in her hands.

"Do you think people will buy them, Mother?" Hershel worried.

"Do onions grow in the ground?" Basha answered. "But we won't sell even one here in the kitchen. I'll bake your cookies, and we'll carry them to market."

The market was already a busy place. Hershel could smell the familiar odor of herring and pickles, bread and cheeses. He could hear the chickens cackling and the vendors calling out. But today there were new, sweet smells coming from the tables loaded with Purim treats: the honey cakes, the bottles of syrups, pears, wines, the hamantashen shaped like Haman's three-cornered hat.

Hershel and Basha set out their baked goods.

"Buy a special cake for Purim!" Basha called.

Soon there was quite a crowd around Basha's table.

Fayge the belt maker wanted four cookies. And Lieba the feather picker wanted three. Even Berel the baker bought a cookie, the last one. He pinched Hershel's cheek as he walked by.

"You'll be a talented baker someday," he said. "Come talk to me."

"Hershel." His mother turned to him. "Did you hear what Berel said? It's not every day a nice word like that comes from his mouth. And every hamantash, every cookie is gone."

Hershel couldn't see the table. But he could feel the excitement all around him. Purim excitement. Cookie excitement. Talent excitement. And in his head, he could see himself as a man, a baker, perhaps, with bowls of flour all around. Or a carpenter, or a shoemaker, or a toolmaker. Oh, how happy Hershel was!

Author's Note

Purim, one of the noisiest and most enjoyable of all Jewish holidays, occurs on the fourteenth day of the Hebrew month of Adar (February or March).

The setting is Ancient Persia. The king, Ahasuerus, has recently chosen a new queen, Esther. She is an orphan who has been raised by her cousin, Mordecai.

Trouble for the Jews begins when Haman, the highest court official, realizes that Mordecai will not bow down to him. In anger, he plots to kill all the Jews of Persia. The king, unaware that Esther is Jewish, grants Haman permission to destroy her people. The word "Purim" comes from the Hebrew word pur, which means "lot," referring to the lots Haman cast to select the date of destruction.

When Mordecai learns of the royal decree, he sends word to Esther. Since no one is allowed to call upon the king unless summoned, Esther risks her life to speak to Ahasuerus. She finds favor with the king and informs him of Haman's intention to kill her people. The tables are turned: the king orders that Haman suffer the fate he had planned for Mordecai and the Jews.

Turning the tables is the order of the day for Purim. People dress up in costumes, perform skits and parodies, eat, drink, and sing. On this joyous holiday, Jews give charity and gifts to the poor, as well as gifts to friends and relatives. These often include the traditional hamantashen, triangular pastries filled with fruit or poppy seeds that resemble Haman's three-cornered hat.